But Jack didn't work hard.

He didn't work at all.

He just liked to eat porridge

and sit in the sun and sleep.

3

One day, Jack's mother said,
"You are very lazy, Jack.
You'll get no more porridge
until you get a job."

# Lazy
# Jack

by Sue Graves and Roger Simó

**W**
FRANKLIN WATTS
LONDON•SYDNEY

Jack lived in an old cottage with his mother.

They were very poor.

Jack's mother worked hard every day.

Jack was cross.

He liked porridge very much.

"Oh, all right, Mother," he said.

"I'll get a job today."

Jack got a job feeding some hens.

The farmer paid him a penny for his work.

Jack was very pleased.

He tossed the penny up in the air.

But it fell into the stream.

Jack told his mother that he had lost

his penny.

"You are a silly boy," said his mother.

"You should have put the penny

in your pocket!"

"That's a good idea," said Jack.

"Next time I will."

The next day, Jack got a job
milking some cows.

The farmer paid him with a pot of milk.

Jack put the pot of milk in his pocket.

But the milk spilled everywhere.

When Jack got home, the milk was gone
and his trousers were all wet.

"You are a silly boy," said his mother.

"You should have put the pot
on your head!"

"I didn't think of that," said Jack.

"I will do that next time."

Jack's next job was making cheese.

The farmer paid him with a big cheese.

Jack put the cheese on his head.

But it was a very hot day

and the cheese began to melt.

Jack's mother was cross.

"You are a silly boy," she said.

"You should have put the cheese

on your shoulder."

Jack looked at his mother.

"You are very clever," he said.

"Next time I will do as you say."

Sometime later, Jack got a job
looking after donkeys.
The farmer paid him with a donkey.
Jack put the donkey on his back.

The donkey was very heavy
and it was hard to carry.
Jack walked home very slowly.
He swayed from side to side as he walked.

The donkey got so heavy that Jack

had to rest. He stopped by a big house

and put the donkey down.

The house belonged to a rich man

and his daughter.

Jack looked through the window

and saw the daughter sitting by the fire.

She looked so sad.

The rich man came to the door.

"Why is your daughter so sad?" asked Jack.

"She cannot hear or speak," said the man.
"The doctors say she will not get better
until somebody makes her laugh.
The first man to make her laugh
can marry her and have all her riches.
People have come here to try, but not one
of them has even made her smile."

"I hope she gets better soon," said Jack.

He picked up the donkey again, and left.

The daughter looked out of the window.

She saw Jack staggering from side to side

and she saw the donkey on his back.

The daughter laughed and laughed
and laughed. It looked so funny.
And now she could hear and speak.
The rich man was very pleased.
"You may marry my daughter," he told Jack.

Jack and the rich man's daughter
got married.

Now Jack was a rich man, too.

Jack's mother was very happy.

She never had to work again.

And neither did Jack.

So they all lived happily ever after.

# Story order

Look at these 5 pictures and captions.
Put the pictures in the right order
to retell the story.

**1**

The donkey was hard to carry.

**2**

Jack marries the rich man's daughter.

**3**

Jack's mother tells Jack to get a job.

**4**

The cheese melts over Jack.

**5**

The rich man's daughter laughed.

# Independent Reading

This series is designed to provide an opportunity for your child to read on their own. These notes are written for you to help your child choose a book and to read it independently.

In school, your child's teacher will often be using reading books which have been banded to support the process of learning to read. Use the book band colour your child is reading in school to help you make a good choice. *Lazy Jack* is a good choice for children reading at Purple Band in their classroom to read independently.

The aim of independent reading is to read this book with ease, so that your child enjoys the story and relates it to their own experiences.

## About the book

In this adaptation of an old English story, Jack's mother orders her lazy son to find a job. But each job Jack tries seems to end in disaster. Will his luck change?

## Before reading

Help your child to learn how to make good choices by asking:

"Why did you choose this book? Why do you think you will enjoy it?"

Look at the cover together and ask: "What do you think the story will be about?" Ask your child to think of what they already know about the story context. Then ask your child to read the title aloud. Ask: "What does the setting and clothing tell you about Jack?"

Remind your child that they can sound out the letters to make a word if they get stuck.

Decide together whether your child will read the story independently or read it aloud to you.

## During reading

Remind your child of what they know and what they can do independently. If reading aloud, support your child if they hesitate or ask for help by telling the word. If reading to themselves, remind your child that they can come and ask for your help if stuck.

## After reading

Support comprehension by asking your child to tell you about the story. Use the story order puzzle to encourage your child to retell the story in the right sequence, in their own words. The correct sequence can be found on the next page.

Help your child think about the messages in the book that go beyond the story and ask: "Why did Jack's mother ask Jack to get a job? How else could Jack have helped? Does this story remind you of any other traditional tales with a character called Jack?"

Give your child a chance to respond to the story: "Did you have a favourite part? Which part did you think was most funny? Why?"

## Extending learning

Help your child think more about the inferences in the story by asking: "Do you think Jack earned his reward? Why/Why not?"

In the classroom, your child's teacher may be teaching how to use speech marks to show when characters are speaking. There are many examples in this book that you could look at with your child. Find these together and point out how the end punctuation (comma, full stop, question mark or exclamation mark) comes inside the speech mark. Ask the child to read some examples out loud, adding appropriate expression.

Franklin Watts
First published in Great Britain in 2018
by The Watts Publishing Group

Copyright © The Watts Publishing Group 2018
All rights reserved.

Series Editors: Jackie Hamley and Melanie Palmer
Series Advisors: Dr Sue Bodman and Glen Franklin
Series Designer: Peter Scoulding

A CIP catalogue record for this book is
available from the British Library.

ISBN 978 1 4451 6236 2 (hbk)
ISBN 978 1 4451 6238 6 (pbk)
ISBN 978 1 4451 6237 9 (library ebook)

Printed in China

Franklin Watts
An imprint of
Hachette Children's Group
Part of The Watts Publishing Group
Carmelite House
50 Victoria Embankment
London EC4Y 0DZ

An Hachette UK Company
www.hachette.co.uk

www.franklinwatts.co.uk

FSC
www.fsc.org
MIX
Paper from
responsible sources
FSC® C104740

**Answer to Story order: 3,4,1,5,2**